Enid

A **FARAWAY TREE**
Adventure

JOE and the
MAGIC SNOWMAN

EGMONT

The World of the FARAWAY TREE

MOON-FACE lives at the very top. In his house is the start of the **SLIPPERY-SLIP**, a huge slide that curves all the way down inside the trunk of the tree.

SILKY lives below Moon-Face. She is the prettiest little fairy you ever did see.

SAUCEPAN MAN is a funny old thing. His saucepans make lots of noise when they jangle together, so he can't hear very well.

CHAPTER ONE
Beth Makes Some Toffee for Moon-Face

The children had talked about nothing else but the Faraway Tree and its strange folk for days. Beth had promised to take toffee to Moon-Face.

'**Promises must never be broken**,' she said. 'I will make some toffee if Mother will let me have the sugar, syrup and milk. Then when it's done you can take it to Moon-Face, Joe.'

Mother said they could make toffee on Wednesday, after she had been to the shops. So on Wednesday Beth set to work making the **best, sweetest, chewiest toffee** she could.

She set it in a pan on the stove. It cooked beautifully. When it had cooled and was set nice and hard, Beth broke it up into small pieces. She put them into a paper bag, gave one piece each to the others, and popped one into her own mouth.

'I'll have to go at **night**, I think,' said Joe. 'I shan't get any time off this week, I know. We're so busy with the garden now.'

So that night, when the **moon was shining brightly** in the sky overhead, Joe slipped out of bed. Beth and Frannie woke up and heard him. They hadn't meant to go with him, but when they saw the moonlight shining everywhere and thought of that exciting Faraway Tree, they felt that they simply couldn't stay behind! **Wouldn't you have felt that too?**

They dressed quickly and whispered through
Joe's door. 'We're coming too, Joe. **Wait for us!**'

Joe waited. Then they all three slipped down
the creaky stairs and out into the moonlit
garden. The shadows were very black indeed,
just like ink. There was no colour anywhere,
only just the **pale, cold moonlight**.

They were soon in the Enchanted Wood.
But, dear me, it was quite, quite different now!
It was **simply alive** with people and animals!
In the very dark parts of the wood little
lanterns were hung in rows. In the moonlit
parts there were no lanterns, and a great deal of
chattering was going on.

Nobody took any notice of the children at all. Nobody seemed surprised to see them. But the children were **most astonished** at everything!

'There's a market over there!' whispered Joe to Beth. 'Look! There are necklaces made of painted acorns and brooches made of wild roses!'

But Beth was looking at something else – a dance going on in the moonlit dell, with fairies and pixies **chattering and laughing** together. Sometimes, when they were tired of dancing on their feet, partners would fly in the air and dance there in the moonlight.

Frannie was watching some elves growing toadstools. As fast as the toadstool grew, an elf laid a cloth on it and put glasses of lemonade and tiny cakes there. It was all like a **strange dream**.

'Oh, I am glad we came!' said Beth, in delight. 'Who would have thought that the Enchanted Wood would be like this at night?'

They wasted a great deal of time looking at everything, but at last they got to the Faraway Tree. And even here there was a great difference! The whole tree was hung with strings of tiny lights and glittered softly from branch to branch, rather like a very enormous **Christmas Tree**.

Joe saw something else. It was a stout rope going from branch to branch, for people to hold on to when they wished to go up the tree.

'Look at that!' he said. 'It will be much easier to go up tonight. All we'll have to do is just to hold on to the rope and pull ourselves up by it! **Come on!**'

Other folk, and some animals too, were going up the tree.

Not to

the land at

the top, but to visit

their friends who lived

in the trunk of the enormous

old tree. All the doors and windows

were open now, and there was a great deal of

laughing and **talking** going on.

The children climbed up and up and came at last to the top. They knocked on Moon-Face's yellow door. 'Come in!' yelled a voice, and in they went.

Moon-Face was sitting on his curved bed, mending one of his cushions. **'Hallo!'** he said. 'Did you bring me that toffee you owe me?'

'Yes,' said Joe, handing him the bag. 'There's a lot there, Moon-Face – half to pay you for last week's slippery-slide, and half to pay you if you'll let us go down again tonight.'

'Oh my!' said Moon-Face, looking with great delight into the bag. **'What lovely toffee!'**

He crammed four large pieces into his mouth and sucked with joy.

'Is it nice?' said Beth.

'**Ooble-ooble-ooble-ooble!**' answered Moon-Face, quite unable to speak properly, for his teeth were all stuck together with the toffee! The children laughed.

'Is the Roundabout Land at the top of the Faraway Tree?' asked Joe.

Moon-Face shook his head. 'Ooooble!' he said.

'What land is there now?' asked Frannie.

Moon-Face made a face, and screwed up his nose. '**Ooooble-ooooble-ooooble-ooooble-ooooble!**' he said very earnestly.

'Oh dear, we shan't be able to get anything out of him at all whilst he's eating toffee,' said Beth. 'He'll just ooble away. What a pity! I would have liked to know what **strange land** was there tonight.'

'I'll just go and peep!' said Joe, jumping up. Moon-Face looked alarmed. He shook his

head, and caught hold of Joe. 'Ooooble-ooooble-
ooooble-ooooble!' he cried.

'It's all right,
Moon-Face,
I'm only
going to
peep,' said
Joe. 'I shan't
go into the
land.'

**'OOBLE-
OOBLE-OOBLE-
OOBLE!'** cried Moon-Face in a fright, trying
his best to swallow all the toffee so that he
could speak properly. 'Ooooble!'

Joe didn't listen. He went out of the door
with the girls, and climbed up the last branch
of the Faraway Tree. What strange land was

above it this time? Joe peered up through
the dark hole in the cloud, through which a
beam of moonlight shone down.

He came to the little ladder that ran up the
hole in the cloud. He climbed up it. His head
poked out into the land at the top. He gave a
shout.

'Beth! Frannie! It's a kind of **ice and snow!**
There are big white bears everywhere! Oh, do
come and look!'

But then a **dreadful thing** happened!
Something lifted Joe right off the ladder – and
he disappeared into the land of ice and snow
above the cloud.

'Come back! Joe, come back!' yelled

Moon-Face, swallowing all his toffee in fright. 'You mustn't even look, or the **Snowman will get you!**'

But Joe was gone. Beth looked at Moon-Face in dismay. 'What shall we do?' she said.

CHAPTER TWO
Joe and the
Magic Snowman

Moon-Face was most upset to see Joe disappear. 'I told him not to – I told him!' he groaned.

'You didn't,' sobbed Frannie. 'Your mouth was full of toffee and all you could say was "Oooble-ooble-ooble!" And how could we know what that meant?'

'Where's Joe now?' asked Beth, quite pale with shock.

Yes, indeed – **where was Joe?** Someone had lifted him right off the ladder, up into the Land of Ice and Snow! And there, strangely enough, the moon and the sun were in the sky at the same time, one at one side and the other opposite, both shining with a pale light.

Joe shivered, for it was very cold. He looked up to see what had lifted him off the ladder, and he saw in front of him a big strange creature – **a snowman!** He was just like the snowmen Joe had so often made in the wintertime – **round and fat and white**, with an old hat stuck on his head and a carrot for a nose.

'This is luck!' said the Snowman, in a **soft, snowy sort of voice**. 'I've been standing by that hole for days, waiting for a seal to come up – and you came!'

'Oh,' said Joe, remembering that seals came up to breathe through holes in the ice.

'That wasn't a waterhole – that was the hole that led down the Faraway Tree. I want to go back, please.'

'The hole has closed up,' said the Snowman. Joe looked – and to his great dismay he saw that a **thick layer of ice** had formed over the hole – so thick that he knew perfectly well he could never break through it.

'Whatever shall I do now?' he said.

'Just what I tell you,' said the Snowman, with a grin. **This is splendid!** In this dull and silent land there is nothing but polar bears and seals and penguins. I have often wanted someone to talk to.'

'How did you get here?' asked Joe,
wrapping his coat firmly round him,
for he was bitterly cold.

'Ah,' said the Snowman, 'that's a long story!
I was made by some children long ago – and
when they had finished me, they laughed at
me and threw stones at me to break me up. So
that night I crept away here – and made myself
King, but **what's the good of being King**
if you've only bears and things to talk to? What
I want is a really good servant who can talk my
language. And now you've come!'

'But I don't want to be your servant,' said Joe indignantly.

'**Nonsense!**' said the Snowman, and he gave Joe a push that nearly sent him over. Then, on big, flat snow-feet he moved forward to where there was a low wall of snow.

'**Make me a good house**,' he said.

'I don't know how to!' said Joe.

'Oh, just cut blocks of this stiff icy snow and build them up one on top of another,' said the Snowman. 'When you've finished I'll give you a warm coat to wear. Then you won't shiver so much.'

Joe didn't see that he could do anything but obey. So he picked up a shovel that was lying by the wall and began to cut **big bricks of the frozen snow**. When he had cut about twenty he stopped and placed them one on top of another till one side of the round house was made. Then he began to cut snow-bricks again, wondering all the time how in the world he would ever be able to escape from this strange land.

Joe had often built little snow-houses of soft snow in his garden at home during the winter. Now he had made a big one, with proper snow-blocks, as hard as bricks. He quite enjoyed it, though **he did wish the girls were there too.** When he had finished it, and made a nice rounded roof, the Snowman came shuffling up.

'Very nice,' he said, '**very nice indeed**. I can just get in, I think.'

He squeezed his big snow-body inside, and threw out a thick coat for Joe, made of wool

as soft and as white as the snow all
around. Joe put it on very thankfully. Then he
tried to squeeze in after the Snowman, for he
wanted to be out of the cold, icy wind.

But he was
so squashed
between the
Snowman and
the walls of
the snow-house
that he couldn't
breathe.

'**Don't push so**,' said the
Snowman disagreeably.
'Move up.'

'I can't!' gasped poor
Joe. He felt quite
certain that he would
be pushed right out
of the snow-hut
through a hole in
the wall!

Just then there came a **curious grunt** at the doorway. The Snowman called out at once.

'Is that you, Furry? Take this boy to your home under the ice. He's a nuisance here. He keeps squashing me!'

Joe looked up to see who Furry was – and he saw a great white bear looking in. The bear had a stupid but kind look on his face.

'Ooomph!' said the bear, and pulled Joe out into the open air. Joe

35

knew it was no use to struggle. Nobody could get away from a bear as big as that! But the bear was certainly very kindly.

'**Oooomph?**' he said to Joe, with a loud grunting noise.

'I don't know what you mean,' said Joe.

The bear said no more. He just took Joe along with him, half carrying the little boy, for Joe found the way very slippery indeed.

CHAPTER THREE
Under the Ice and Snow

They came to a hole that led under the ice and snow. The bear pushed Joe down it – and to Joe's enormous surprise he found there was a big room underneath, with five bears there, big and little! It was **quite warm there too** – Joe was astonished, for there was no heater, of course.

'Ooomph,' said all the bears politely.

'Ooomph!' said Joe. **That pleased the
bears very much indeed**. They came
and shook paws with Joe very solemnly and
oomphed all over him.

Joe liked the look of the bears much more
than he liked the look of the Snowman. He

thought perhaps they might help him to escape from this silly land of ice and snow.

'Could you tell me the way back to the Faraway Tree?' he asked the bears politely and clearly.

The bears looked at one another and then **ooomphed** at Joe. It was quite clear that they didn't understand a word he said.

'Never mind,' said Joe, with a sigh, and made up his mind to put up with things till he could see a way to escape.

The Snowman was a great nuisance. No sooner did Joe settle himself down for a nap, leaning his head against the **big warm body** of a bear, than there came a call from the snow-house.

'**Hey, boy!** Come here and play dominoes with me!'

So Joe had to go and play dominoes, and as the Snowman wouldn't let him come into the house because he said he was squashed, Joe had to sit at the doorway and play, and he nearly froze to bits.

Then another time, just as he was eating a nice bit of fried fish that one of the bears had kindly cooked for him, the Snowman shouted to him to come and make him a window in his house.

And Joe had to hurry off and cut a sheet of clear ice to fit into one side of the snow-house for a window! **Really, that Snowman was a perfect nuisance!**

I wish to goodness I'd never stepped into this silly land, thought Joe a hundred times. It's a good thing the bears are so nice to me. I only wish they could say something else besides '**Ooomph**.'

43

Joe wondered what Beth and Frannie were doing. Were they very upset when he didn't come back? Would they go home and tell their father and mother what had happened?

Beth and Frannie **were** upset! It had been **dreadful** to see poor Joe disappear through the cloud like that.

Moon-Face looked very solemn too. He could speak quite well now that he had swallowed all his toffee.

'We must rescue him,' he said, his face shining like the full moon.

'How?' asked the girls.

'I must think,' said Moon-Face, and he shut his eyes. His **head swelled up** with his thinking. He opened his eyes and nodded his head.

'We'll go to Goldilocks and the Three Bears,' he said. 'Her bears know the Land of Ice and Snow. She might be able to help Joe that way.'

'But where does Goldilocks live?' asked Beth, in wonder. 'I thought she was just a fairy tale.'

'**Good gracious, no!**' said Moon-Face. 'Come on – we'll have to catch the train.'

'What train?' asked Frannie, in astonishment.

'Oh, wait and see!' said Moon-Face. 'Hurry now – go down the slippery-slip and wait for me at the bottom!'

CHAPTER FOUR
The House of the Three Bears

Beth took a cushion, put it at
the top of the slide, and pushed
off. Down she went, **whizzzzzzz!**
She shot to the bottom, flew out of
the trapdoor and landed on the cushion
of moss. She had hardly got up before Frannie

flew out of the trapdoor too.

'You know, that slippery-slip is the **greatest fun!**' said Beth. 'I'd like to do that all day long!'

'Yes, if only we didn't have to climb all the way up the tree first,' said Frannie.

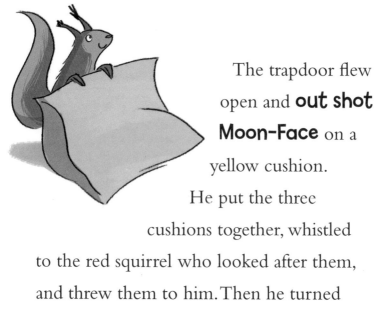

The trapdoor flew open and **out shot Moon-Face** on a yellow cushion. He put the three cushions together, whistled to the red squirrel who looked after them, and threw them to him. Then he turned to the waiting girls.

'There's a train at **midnight**,' he said. 'We shall have to hurry.'

The wood was still bright with moonlight. The three of them hurried between the trees. Suddenly Beth heard the **chuffing** of a train, and she and Frannie stopped in surprise. They saw a small train winding in and out of the trees, looking for all the world like an old-fashioned **clockwork toy train** made big! The engine even had a key in its side – as if to wind it up!

There was a **small station** nearby.
Moon-Face caught hold of the girls' hands and
ran to it. The train was standing quite still there.

The carriages had tin doors and windows which didn't open, just like those of a clockwork train. Beth tried her hardest to open a door, but it was no use. The train whistled. It was anxious to be off.

'Don't you know how to get into this train?' asked Moon-Face, with a laugh. 'You are sillies! **You just slide the roof off!**'

As he spoke he pushed at the roof – and it slid off like the roof of a toy train's carriage.

'I think this is just a toy clockwork train made big,' said Frannie, climbing over the side of the carriage and getting in at the roof. '**I never saw such a funny train in my life!**'

They all got in. Moon-Face couldn't seem to slide the roof on again properly, so he stood up inside the carriage, and when the train went off, Beth and Frannie, who couldn't possibly see out of the tin windows, stood up and looked out of the roof instead. **They did look funny!**

At the next station, which was
called '**Dolls' Station**', three dolls
got into the carriage and stared at them
very hard. One was so like Beth's own doll
at home that she couldn't help staring back.
The second station was called '**Crosspatch
Station**', and standing next to the railway
tracks were three of the crossest-looking old
women that the girls had ever seen. One of
them got into their carriage, and the three

dolls at once got out, and climbed into the
next one.

'**Move up!**' said the Crosspatch angrily to
Moon-Face. He moved up.

The Crosspatch was an uncomfortable
person to travel with. She grumbled all the
time, and her basket, which was full of prickly
bunches of roses, kept bumping into poor
Frannie.

'**Here we are, here we are!**' sang out Moon-Face, when they got to the next station, and the three of them got out gladly, leaving the Crosspatch grumbling away all to herself.

The station was called 'Bears' Station', and there were a **great many teddy bears** about, some brown, some pink, some blue, and some white. When they wanted to talk to one another they kept pressing themselves in the middle, where the button that made them talk was, and then they could talk quite well. Frannie wanted to giggle when she saw them doing this. It did look so funny.

'Please could you tell me the way to the Three Bears' House?' Moon-Face asked a blue teddy bear politely.

The bear pressed himself in the middle and answered in a **nice growly voice**, 'Up the lane and down the lane and around the lane.'

'Thank you,' said Moon-Face.

'It sounds a bit funny to me,' said Beth doubtfully.

'**Not at all,**' said Moon-Face, led leading them up a little lane through the honeysuckle. 'Here we are, going up a lane – and now you see it goes downhill – so we're going down – and presently we'll turn a corner and go around the lane!'

He was right. They went up and then down and then around – and there in front of them, tucked into a woody corner, was the **dearest, prettiest little house** the girls had ever seen! It was **covered with pink roses** from top to bottom, and its tiny windows winked in the moonlight as if they had eyes.

Moon-Face knocked at the door. A sleepy voice cried, 'Come in!' Moon-Face opened the door and they all went in. There was a table in front of them, and on it were three steaming bowls of what some people call porridge, and some call oatmeal, and round it were three chairs, one big, one middle-sized, and one tiny.

'It's the House of the Three Bears all right!' whispered Beth excitedly. **It was just like seeing a fairy story come true!**

'We're here!' said the voice from another room. Moon-Face went in with Beth and Frannie. The other room was a small bedroom, with a big bed in it, a middle-sized bed, and in the cot was **a most adorable baby bear** with the bluest eyes the girls had ever seen.

'Where's Goldilocks?' asked Moon-Face.

'Gone shopping,' said the father bear.

'Where does she sleep when she's here?' asked Beth, looking round. 'And does she always live with you now?'

'Always,' said the father bear, putting his big nightcap straight. 'She looks after us very well. There's a market on tonight in the Enchanted Wood and she's gone to see if she can buy some porridge cheap. As for where she sleeps, well, she just chooses any of our beds, you know, and we **cuddle up together** then. But she likes the baby bear's bed best, because it's **so soft and warm**.'

'She did in the story,' said Frannie.

'What story?' asked the mother bear.

'Well – the story of the Three Bears,' said Frannie.

'Never heard of it,' said the Three Bears, all together, which really seemed rather extraordinary to Beth and Frannie. They didn't like to ask any more questions after that.

'Here's Goldilocks now!' said the mother bear. The sound of a **little high voice** could be heard coming nearer and nearer. The baby bear sprang out of his cot and ran to the door in delight.

A pretty little girl with long, curling golden hair picked him up and hugged him. **'Hallo, dearest!'** she said. 'Have you been a good bear?'

Then she saw Beth, Frannie and Moon-Face, and stared at them in surprise.

'Who are you?' she said.

Moon-Face explained about Joe, and how he had gone to the Land of Ice and Snow, where the big white bears lived.

'I'm afraid the Magic Snowman will make him a prisoner there,' said Moon-Face. 'And he'll have to live with the white bears. Could you get your Three Bears to come with us and ask the white bears to let Joe go free, Goldilocks?'

'But I don't know the way,' said Goldilocks.

'**We do!**' said the father bear suddenly. 'The white bears are cousins of ours. Moon-Face, if you can help us with a little bit of magic, we can visit the Land of Ice and Snow in a few minutes!'

'**Good gracious!**' said Beth, most astonished. 'But it's ever so far away, right at the top of the Faraway Tree!'

'That doesn't matter,' said the father bear. He took down a large jar from the mantelpiece and filled it with water. He put into it a yellow powder and stirred it with a **big black crow's feather**.

Moon-Face put his hands into the water and began to sing a string of such strange words that Beth and Frannie felt quite **trembly**. The water bubbled. It rose up to the top of the jar. It overflowed and ran on to the floor. It turned to ice beneath their feet! A cold wind filled the little house and everyone shivered.

Then Beth looked out of the window —
and what she saw there filled her with such
amazement that she couldn't say a word, but
just pointed.

Frannie looked too — and **whatever do
you think?** Outside lay nothing but ice and
snow — they were in the same land as Joe!
Though how this land happened neither Beth
nor Frannie could make out.

'We're there,' said Moon-Face, taking his hands out of the jar and drying them on his red handkerchief. 'Can you lend us any coats, bears? We shall be cold here.'

The mother bear handed them thick coats out of a cupboard. They put them on. The bears already had thick fur and did not need anything extra.

'Now to go and find Joe!' said Moon-Face. 'Come on, bears – **you've got to help!**'

CHAPTER FIVE
The Battle of the Bears

Goldilocks, the Three Bears, the girls, and Moon-Face all went out of the little cottage. How strange it seemed to see **roses blossoming** over the walls, when ice and snow lay all around!

'The thing is – where do we go to find the polar bears?' said Goldilocks.

'Over there, towards the sun,' said the father bear. Beth and Frannie were surprised to see both the moon and the sun shining in the sky. They followed the father bear, **slipping** and **sliding**, and holding on to one another. It was very cold, and their noses and toes felt as if they were freezing.

Suddenly they saw the **little snow-house** that Joe had built for the Magic Snowman.

'Look!' said the father bear. 'We'd better make for that.'

But before they got there a big white figure

squeezed itself out of the snow-house and saw

them. **It was the Magic Snowman!** As soon

as he saw the Three Bears and the others, he

began to shout loudly in a windy, snowy voice:

'**Enemies! Enemies!** Hey, bears, come and send off the enemies!'

'We're not enemies,' yelled Moon-Face, and Goldilocks ran forward to show the Snowman that she was a little girl. But Moon-Face pulled her back. He didn't trust that old Snowman!

The Snowman bent his big fat body down and picked up **great handfuls of snow**. He threw one at Goldilocks. She ducked down, and it passed over her and hit the baby bear.

'**Oooooch!**' he said, and sat down in a hurry. Then everything happened at once. A crowd of white polar bears hurried out of their underground home to help the Snowman, and soon the air was full of flying snowballs.

The snow was hard, and the balls hurt when they hit anyone. It wasn't a bit of good the girls shouting that they were friends, not enemies. Nobody heard them, and soon

there was a **fierce battle** going on!

'Oh dear!' gasped Beth, trying her best to throw straight. '**This is dreadful!** We shall never rescue Joe by behaving like this!'

But there really didn't
seem anything else to
be done! After all, if
people are fighting
you, you can't do much
but defend yourself, and
the Three Bears, and the girls,
and Moon-Face felt very angry at having hard
snowballs thrown at them.

Smack! Thud! Biff! Squish! The snowballs
burst as they hit, and soon
there was a great
noise of angry
'Ooomphs' from
the white bears,
and **'Oooches'**
from the Three
Bears, and yells

from the children, and screeches from Moon-Face, who acted as if he was mad, hopping about and yelling and kicking up the snow as well as throwing it! His big round face was a fine target for snowballs, and he was hit more than anybody else. **Poor Moon-Face!**

Now whilst this fierce battle was going on, where do you suppose Joe was?

As soon as he heard
the cry of 'Enemies!
Enemies!' he had hidden in
a corner, for he didn't want to be
mixed up in any fight. When he saw
the white bears going out, and he was left
all alone, he began at once to think
of escaping.

He crept to the hole that led above-ground.
The battle was some way off, so Joe did not
see that the enemies were really his own
friends! If he had he would have gone to join
them at once.

What a **terrible noise** they are all making!

he thought. It sounds like a **battle between gorillas** and bears to me! I'm not going near them – I'd be eaten up or something! I shall just run hard the opposite way and hope I'll meet someone to help me.

So Joe, dressed in his big white woolly coat, and looking **just like a little white bear himself**, crept off over the ice and snow, not seen by anyone. He ran as soon as he thought he was out of sight. He ran and he ran and he ran.

But he met nobody. Not
a soul was to be seen. Only
a lonely seal lay on a shelf
of ice, but even he dived
below as soon as he saw Joe.

And then Joe stopped
in the **greatest
astonishment** and stared
as if his eyes would fall out
of his head. He had come
to the cottage of the Three Bears, standing all
alone in the middle of the ice and snow – and,
of course, its roses were still blooming round it,
scenting the air.

'**I'm dreaming!**' said Joe. 'I simply must be
dreaming! A cottage – with roses – here in the
middle of the snow! Well – I shall go and see
who lives there. Perhaps they would give me

something to eat and let me rest, for I'm very hungry and tired.'

He knocked at the door. There was no answer. He opened the door and went in. **How he stared!** There was no one to be seen at all, but on the table stood **three bowls of steaming porridge**, one big, one middle-sized, and one small. It was rather dark, so Joe lighted a big candle on the table.

Then he sank down into the biggest chair –
but it was far too big and he got up again. He
sat down in the next sized chair – but that was
too piled up with cushions, and he got up to
sit in the smallest chair. That was **just right**,
and Joe settled down comfortably – but alas,
his weight was too much for it, and the chair
broke to bits beneath him!

He looked at the delicious porridge. He
tasted the porridge in the biggest bowl – it was
much too hot and burnt his tongue.

He tasted the next bowl – but that was far too sweet. But when he tasted the porridge in the little bowl, it was **just right**.

So Joe ate it all up! Then he felt **so sleepy** that he thought he really must rest. So he went into the bedroom and lay down on the biggest bed. But it was far too big, so he tried the middle-sized one. That was too soft and went down in the middle, so Joe lay down on the cot. And that was **so small and warm and comfortable** that he fell fast asleep!

All this time the snowball battle was going on. The Snowman was so big and the polar bears were so fierce that very soon the Three Bears, the children, and Moon-Face were driven backwards.

Then a **snowstorm** blew up, and the snow fell so thickly that it was quite impossible to see anything. Moon-Face called out in **alarm**:

'Bears! Goldilocks! Beth! Frannie! Take hold of each others' hands at once and don't let go. **One of us might easily be lost in the storm!**'

Everyone at once took hands. The snow blew into their faces and they could see nothing. Bending forwards they began to walk carefully away from the white bears, who had stopped fighting now and were trying to find out where their enemies were.

'Don't shout or anything,' said Moon-Face. 'We don't want the white bears to hear us, in case they take us prisoners. They might not listen to the Three Bears. Move off, and we'll look for some sort of shelter till this storm is over.'

They were all very miserable. They were cold, rather frightened, and quite lost. They stumbled over the snow, keeping hold of one another's hands firmly. They went on and on, and suddenly Goldilocks shook off Moon-Face's hand and pointed in front of them.

'**A light!**' she said in astonishment. Everyone stopped.

'**I say! I SAY!** It's our cottage!' shrieked the baby bear, in surprise and delight. 'But who's inside? Someone must have lighted the candle!'

They all stared at the lighted window. Who was inside the cottage? Could the Magic Snowman have found it? Or the polar bears? Was it an enemy inside – or a friend?

'**Wheeeeew!**' blew the wind, and the snowflakes fell thickly on everyone as they stood there, wondering.

'**Ooooh!**' shivered Moon-Face. 'We shall get dreadful colds standing out here in the snow. Let's go in, and find out who's there.'

So the father bear opened the door, and one by one they all trooped in, looking round the empty room, half afraid.

CHAPTER SIX
More and More Surprises

'There doesn't seem to be anyone here!' said Beth, cautiously looking around.

'**Well, WHO lighted that candle?**' asked Moon-Face, his big round face looking anxious. 'We didn't leave it burning!'

Suddenly the father bear gave an angry growl, and pointed to his chair. '**Who's been sitting in my chair?**' he said.

'And who's been sitting in my chair?' said
the mother bear, pointing to hers.

**'And who's been sitting in my chair
and broken it all to**

bits?' squeaked the
baby bear, in tears.
Beth giggled.
'This sounds
like the story of
the Three Bears
coming true!' she
said to Frannie.

'They'll talk about porridge next.'
They did.

'Who's been eating my porridge?' said
the father bear angrily.

'And who's been eating my porridge?' said
the mother bear.

'**And who's been eating mine, and gobbled it all UP?**' wept the baby bear, scraping his spoon round the empty plate.

'It's all very mysterious,' said Moon-Face. 'Somebody lighted the candle – somebody sat in the chairs – somebody ate the porridge. But who?'

'**Not me this time**,' said Goldilocks. 'I was with you all the time we were snowballing, wasn't I, Bears?'

'You certainly were,' growled the father bear softly, patting the little girl on the back. He was very fond of her.

'I wish we had found poor Joe,' said Beth.

'Whatever will he be doing in this horrid cold land?'

'Do you suppose we ought to go out and look for him again?' said Frannie, shivering as she thought of the ice-cold wind outside.

'No,' said Moon-Face decidedly. 'No one is going out of this cottage again till we're safely in the wood at home. **I'm afraid we can't**

possibly rescue Joe now.'

'What's that noise?' said Goldilocks suddenly.
Everybody listened. **Someone was snoring
softly in the next room!**

'We never thought of looking there,' said
Moon-Face. 'Who can it be?'

'Shh!' said Goldilocks. 'If we can catch him
asleep, we can hold him tight and he won't be

93

able to get away. But if he wakes up he might be fierce.'

They tiptoed to the door of the bedroom. One by one they squeezed through.

'**Who's been lying on my bed?**' said the father bear, in a growly voice.

'Shh!' said Moon-Face crossly.

'Who's been lying on my bed?' said the mother bear.

'**Shh!**' said everyone.

'**And who's been lying on my bed and is fast asleep there still?**' said the baby bear.

Everyone stared at the cot. Yes – there was someone there – someone covered in white. Was it a polar bear?

'**It's a white bear!**' said Moon-Face, half frightened.

'Let's lock him in before he wakes,' said
the father bear. 'He might still think we are
enemies!'

They all rushed out of the little room and
slammed the door shut with a loud **bang**,
locking it behind them.

'He's caught!' said Moon–Face joyfully.

Joe awoke with a jump. Who had locked
him in? Had the Magic Snowman caught
him again? **He began to shout and bang
on the door**. And then Beth and Frannie
recognised his voice and yelled out loudly:

'Moon-Face! It's Joe! It's Joe! It's Joe! Oh, it's Joe!'

They rushed to the door and unlocked it, and flung their arms around Joe. The boy was too astonished to speak. He hugged his sisters.

'How did you get here?' he asked.

'How did you get here?' cried Beth and Frannie.

'Come into the kitchen and we'll all have some hot porridge and milk,' said Goldilocks. 'We can talk then and get warm.'

So Joe went with the others, all chattering loudly about everything. Goldilocks ladled out porridge into blue bowls, and made some hot chocolate. **Soon everyone was putting sugar on porridge and drinking the hot chocolate.**

Joe poured some milk over his porridge and smiled joyfully at everybody.

'What an adventure this has been!' he said. 'Shall I tell my tale first, or will you tell yours?'

The FARAWAY TREE Adventures

Enid Blyton
A FARAWAY TREE Adventure
A colour short story illustrated by Alex Paterson
The Land of BIRTHDAYS

Enid Blyton
A FARAWAY TREE Adventure
A colour short story illustrated by Alex Paterson
The Land of MAGIC MEDICINES

Enid Blyton
A FARAWAY TREE Adventure
A colour short story illustrated by Alex Paterson
The Land of DO-AS-YOU-PLEASE

Enid Blyton
A FARAWAY TREE Adventure
A colour short story illustrated by Alex Paterson
The Land of TOYS

Enid Blyton
A FARAWAY TREE Adventure
A colour short story illustrated by Alex Paterson
The Land of ENCHANTMENTS